LITTLE WITCH

JULIETTE MacIVER

ILLUSTRATED BY
CAT CHAPMAN

WALKER BOOKS

For Safia, my own Little Witch; and Louis,
Ari and Remy, my Little Wizards.
JM
For my largely wonderful and little bit
wicked sister, Kylie.
CC

First published in Great Britain 2013 by Walker Books Ltd
87 Vauxhall Walk, London SE11 5HJ

2 4 6 8 10 9 7 5 3 1

Text © 2012 Juliette MacIver
Illustrations © 2012 Cat Chapman

The right of Juliette MacIver and Cat Chapman to be identified as author
and illustrator respectively of this work has been asserted by them in
accordance with the Copyright, Designs and Patents Act 1988

This book has been typeset in Bembo Educational

Printed and bound in China

British Library Cataloguing in Publication Data:
a catalogue record for this book is
available from the British Library

ISBN 978-1-4063-5334-1

www.walker.co.uk

The Wonderful Sorceress
5

The Magic Word
25

Wixed Up Merds
45

The Wonderful Sorceress

Mother Witch stood in front of the bathroom mirror, powdering her wart.

"Where are you going, Mummy?" asked Little Witch.

"To the Witches and Wizards' Moon Dance," said Mother Witch. "It's a full moon tonight." She picked up a small frog and rubbed it lightly across her eyelids, leaving a lovely green streak.

"Can I come?" begged Little Witch.

"No, my darling," said Mother Witch, painting her lips with a stick of bats' blood. "Sorceress Monda Green is coming to look after you."

Little Witch pouted. "Sorceress Monda is weird," she said.

"Sorceress Monda is a *wonderful* person, Little Witch. She is just a bit hard of hearing, that's all. You need to remember to speak loudly so she can hear you properly."

Just then the doorbell rang and
Sorceress Monda swept into the house,
leaving a trail of sparkles swirling in the
air behind her.

"How's my Little Witchy-pie?" cooed
Sorceress Monda, scooping Little Witch
up in her arms. "Are you ready to have
some fun?"

Little Witch smiled.

"Now," said Mother Witch to Sorceress Monda, "Baby Wizard is already asleep–"

"Come on, love," called Daddy Wizard, getting the double broomstick out of the cupboard. "Sorceress Monda will be fine. We don't want to be late."

"Be a good girl," said Mother Witch to Little Witch. She kissed her goodbye and whispered, "Don't forget to speak up." Then she and Daddy Wizard set off.

"Can we play dragons and princesses?" Little Witch asked. "I'll be the princess and you be the dragon. You capture me, and I scream and I scream—"

"An *ice-cream*?" cried the Sorceress. "Certainly, my dear. What flavour? How about lemon and slime?"

KAZAM!

An enormous lemon-and-slime ice-cream with crunchy spider sprinkles appeared in Little Witch's hand.

"Yum," she said, and she ate the whole thing.

Soon Little Witch was feeling a little
sick.

"Now," called Sorceress Monda, "it's
time for your bath."

"I don't want a bath," said Little
Witch, sulkily.

"Come, Princess," said Sorceress
Monda. "Your dragon will make you a
bubble bath."

"OK," said Little Witch, brightening. "Can I have heaps of bubbles?"

"*Pizza bubbles*?" said Sorceress Monda. "Never heard of them. Well, I suppose I can do that."

KAZAM!

The bath was full of big, round floating pizzas.

Little Witch was amazed.
When she got out of the
bath, she was covered in bits
of cheese and tomato sauce.
She pulled on her nightie
and ran into the lounge.

It was well
past bedtime
and Little Witch
was having a
marvellous time.

"Watch this, Sorceress Monda," she called, putting on some slippery socks and running down the hall. "I can do floor sliding."

"*Horseriding?*" said Sorceress Monda. "Inside? Well, I suppose there is room for a small unicorn."

KAZAM!

A beautiful black unicorn appeared in the middle of the lounge.

Little Witch was thrilled.

Just after midnight, Mother Witch and Daddy Wizard came home. When they came in the door, they found a puddle of ice-cream on the floor, a huge pile of soggy pizzas in the bath, Little Witch cantering around the lounge on a black unicorn, and ...

Sorceress Monda fast asleep.

"Little Witch!" Mother Witch scolded. "I expected more from you."

"But Mummy!" pleaded Little Witch, sliding off the unicorn. "It wasn't… I didn't…" But it was very hard to explain. "None of it was my idea!"

"Oh, really?" said Daddy Wizard. "Whose idea was it then?"

"Sorceress Monda's," said Little Witch.

"I find that rather hard to believe," said Mother Witch.

Little Witch tried again. "You know how Sorceress Monda doesn't hear some things?"

"*A dozen fearsome things?*" shrieked Sorceress Monda, waking up all of a sudden. "We're surrounded. Run for your life!" And she leaped off the couch and fled from the house.

Little Witch, Mother Witch and Daddy Wizard stared after her. Then they all burst out laughing.

Mother Witch sat down on the couch and drew Little Witch onto her knee.

"I guess you were right," she said. "Sorceress Monda *is* a little weird."

"No, you were right," said Little Witch. "She is *wonderful.*"

The Magic Word

Little Witch was having
toadflakes for breakfast.

"I don't like toadflakes," she said,
pushing the bowl away.

"Well," said Mother Witch calmly,
"that's what you're having. Eat up."

Little Witch scowled. "I want some
milk on it," she said.

"What's the magic word?" asked
Mother Witch.

"ALAKAZAM!" said Little Witch.
The bowl of toadflakes turned into a
bowl of marshmallows.

"That is *not* the magic word," said
Mother Witch. "The magic word is
please."

"Please," said Little Witch.

Mother Witch poured milk over
Little Witch's marshmallows. Then she
turned them back into toadflakes.

"Hey!" said Little Witch.

"Eat up," said Mother Witch. "Mrs Wicked will be here soon to pick you up for school."

Little Witch said goodbye to Mother Witch and Baby Wizard (who had mashed newts all through his hair), and ran outside.

Down flew Mrs Wicked on her broomstick. Little Witch's best friend, Billy Wicked, was riding on the back.

"I want to go on the front!" called Little Witch.

"Well then, what's the magic word?" said Mrs Wicked.

"ALAKAZAM!" said Little Witch.

Mrs Wicked's broomstick turned into a cow.

"Little Witch," cried Mrs Wicked, "that is *not* the magic word!"

"Sorry," mumbled Little Witch, "I didn't mean to."

"The magic word is *please*," said Mrs Wicked.

She tried to turn the cow back into a broomstick.

"Abracadang it," she muttered. "I can't change it back. It seems you have inherited your mother's powers, Little Witch." She sighed. "We're running late. We'll just have to go like this."

Little Witch climbed onto the cow behind Billy Wicked and off they flew!

It was fun flying on
a cow for a change. People
everywhere were looking up
and pointing. Little Witch waved
to them. Billy was embarrassed.
He hid inside his
pointy hat.

When they arrived at school, a group of goblins gathered around Billy.

"Billy lost his broomstick!" they teased. "Billy rides a flying cow!"

They cackled and howled and danced around him.

"Stop that," said Little Witch sternly.

"Make us," shrieked the goblins, and one of them grabbed Billy's schoolbag and danced away with it.

"Give that back," yelled Little Witch.

"What's the magic word?" the goblin sneered.

"ALAKAZAM!" shouted Little Witch.

All five goblins turned into slimy green toads.

Little Witch stared in surprise.

"That is *not* the magic word," came an angry voice from one of the toads. "The magic word is *please*."

"Change us back into goblins," cried the other toads.

"I don't know how," said Little Witch.

"The magic word!" pleaded the toads. "Say the magic word!"

"OK," said Little Witch.
"But you'd better not be mean
to Billy again."

"We won't! We won't!" sobbed
the toads.

Little Witch pointed at the toads
and said ... "PLEASE!"

Nothing happened.

"That's funny," said Little Witch.
"*Everyone* says the magic word is please."

Just then the bell rang and it was time for class.

"Oh, well, see you after school," called Little Witch, and she and Billy went into class.

After school, the toads were still sitting miserably on the grass.

"Little Witch!" they screeched. "It's home time. You have to change us back into goblins."

"What's the magic word?" said Little Witch.

"Please!" cried the toads all together.

"That is *not* the magic word," Little Witch told them. "We did the *real* magic word

in witchcraft lessons today. The real
magic word is ... ALAKAZAM!"

And all five toads turned back into
goblins. Off they ran, as fast as
they could.

"And don't do it again!"
Little Witch called after them.

At bedtime that night, Little Witch snuggled into Mother Witch.

"Mummy," she said, "please is not a magic word."

"Why do you say that, darling?" asked Mother Witch.

"It doesn't change toads back into goblins," said Little Witch, sleepily.

"No," said Mother Witch, "I don't suppose it does. But it does make some things happen."

"When you ask someone to do something for you?" murmured Little Witch.

"That's right," said Mother Witch. "Now off to sleep." Then she added softly, "Please."

Wixed Up Merds

45

*I*n Little Witch's house there was a spells room. Children were not allowed in.

But today, Daddy Wizard had left the door slightly ajar. Little Witch couldn't help having a little look.

She gasped as she slipped into the room. It was dark, with stars sparkling all over the walls, and she could hear the faint hum and crackle of magic.

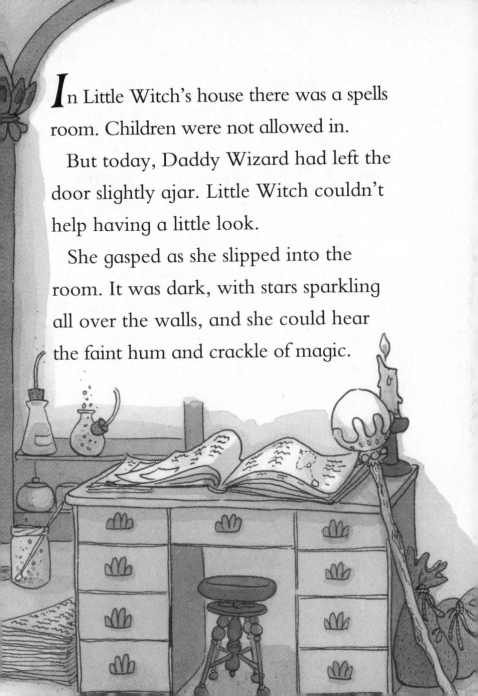

The huge *Book of Spells* lay open on the desk. Little Witch climbed onto the stool, steadying herself with one hand on Daddy Wizard's magic staff. Then, under her breath, she read aloud a spell, "Mumble, mutter, grumble, gutter. Wix up all the merds I utter."

There was a flash of light and Little Witch felt a tingling in her lips.

Just then, the doorbell rang.

"Yoo-hoo," called Mrs Wicked. "Anyone home?"

The staff fell to the floor as Little
Witch ran out of the room.

Little Witch's friend Billy Wicked
had come to play. He and Little Witch
loved to play shops.

"Do you want to shay plops?" she
asked.

"What do you mean?" said Billy.

Little Witch frowned. Why doesn't
Billy understand me? she thought.
We always make a shop. We could
sell magic treasures.

"Let's sell tragic measures," she said.

"You're being silly," said Billy. "I don't want to play." He went off to the kitchen.

Mother Witch and
Mrs Wicked were having
a cup of witch-hazel tea.

"Little Witch is talking
wacky," said Billy.

"I am not walking tacky,"
said Little Witch.

"Little Witch," said Mother
Witch, "stop being silly."

"I am not seeing Billy!"
cried Little Witch.

"Billy is right here,"
said Billy's mother,
helpfully.

"I'm not *booking* for Lilly!" said Little
Witch. She turned to her friend. "Bet's
go, Lilly," she said. "Let's bride our
roomsticks."

Billy shrugged.
"OK," he said.

They crept
past Baby
Wizard's
room.

"Shh," said Little Witch. "Baby Slizard is going to weep."

"What?" said Billy.

"Baby Bizard is in wed," said Little Witch.

Billy looked at her strangely.

Little Witch tried again. "Baby Drizard is just slopping off to weep," she explained.

Out in the garden, Mr Magician was visiting. He had a lot of white rabbits to feed, so Daddy Wizard was picking carrots for him.

"Are you kicking parrots, Daddy?" asked Little Witch.

"Pardon?" said Daddy Wizard.

How strange. Why didn't Daddy know what she was saying?

"Why don't you sow what I'm neighing?" she asked.

"I am going to sow stinging nettles and puffballs," said Daddy Wizard, showing her the seeds.

"I don't like pinging nettles and stuffballs," said Little Witch. What she *did* like was poison apples, picked straight from a poison-apple tree.

"Can we plant a troison-apple pee?" she asked.

"A troison-apple pee?"
said Daddy Wizard.
"What the hex is that?"
Little Witch frowned.
Billy climbed on his
broomstick. "Race you to
the gargoyle!" he said.
Little Witch leaped onto
her broomstick. Up she flew,
waving bye to Daddy. "Die, Baddie,"
she called over her shoulder.
Daddy Wizard looked up. "Come
back here, Little Witch," he called.
Little Witch flew back down.

"What did you just
say to me?" he said.

Little Witch was puzzled. "I
said *dee you later, Saddy*," she said.

Daddy Wizard put down his hoe.
"Have you been in my spells room?"
he asked.

Little Witch went pink.

"Little Witch," said Daddy Wizard,
"I think you have cast a spell on
yourself."

Oh! So *that* was why no one had
understood her today, she thought.

"Wait here," said Daddy Wizard,
and he went into the house.

Then out he came with his magic
staff in his hand. He pointed it at
Little Witch and muttered some magic
words. There was a flash of light and
Little Witch felt that tingling in her lips
again.

"There," said Daddy Wizard. "Your
words will not be mixed up any more."

"Dank you, Thaddy," said
Little Witch.

Daddy Wizard's eyebrows shot up. "It hasn't worked!" he said, giving his staff a shake.

"Just kidding, Daddy," said Little Witch, with a sheepish smile.

Daddy Wizard laughed. "You, my darling, are too clever for words."